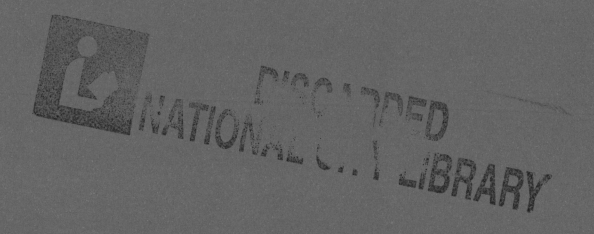

Nothing But a Dog

Perfect Pets

NEW

BOBBI KATZ ❋ *illustrated by* JANE MANNING

Dutton ... Inc.

☆ DUTTON CHILDREN'S BOOKS ☆

A division of Penguin Young Readers Group

PUBLISHED BY THE PENGUIN GROUP ☆ Penguin Group (USA) Inc., 375 Hudson Street, New York, New York 10014, U.S.A. ☆ Penguin Group (Canada), 90 Eglinton Avenue East, Suite 700, Toronto, Ontario M4P 2Y3, Canada (a division of Pearson Penguin Canada Inc.) ☆ Penguin Books Ltd, 80 Strand, London WC2R 0RL, England ☆ Penguin Ireland, 25 St Stephen's Green, Dublin 2, Ireland (a division of Penguin Books Ltd) ☆ Penguin Group (Australia), 250 Camberwell Road, Camberwell, Victoria 3124, Australia (a division of Pearson Australia Group Pty Ltd) ☆ Penguin Books India Pvt Ltd, 11 Community Centre, Panchsheel Park, New Delhi - 110 017, India ☆ Penguin Group (NZ), 67 Apollo Drive, Rosedale, North Shore 0632, New Zealand (a division of Pearson New Zealand Ltd) ☆ Penguin Books (South Africa) (Pty) Ltd, 24 Sturdee Avenue, Rosebank, Johannesburg 2196, South Africa ☆ Penguin Books Ltd, Registered Offices: 80 Strand, London WC2R 0RL, England

Text copyright © 1972 by Bobbi Katz

Illustrations copyright © 2010 by Jane Manning

Text originally published by The Feminist Press.

All rights reserved.

CIP Data available.

Published in the United States by Dutton Children's Books, a division of Penguin Young Readers Group

345 Hudson Street, New York, New York 10014 ☆ www.penguin.com/youngreaders

Designed by Heather Wood with Jane Manning

ISBN: 978-0-525-47858-4

Manufactured in China ☆ First Edition

1 3 5 7 9 10 8 6 4 2

FOR LORI AND FOR EVERY GIRL
WHO HAS EVER WANTED A DOG
—*BK*

FOR DOTTIE,
WITH LOVE
—*JM*

ONCE IT STARTS

—the longing for a dog—

there is no cure for it.

Not an impy squirrel,
Or a parakeet that sings,

Not a fat bunny called Floyd,
Or a kitten that cuddles close and purrs.
Nothing really stops it for very long.

When you are playing checkers and **clump,**
clump,
CLUMP,
You jump doubles!

When you are skating and make a perfect figure eight with no wobbles!

When the wind catches your kite just right
and you feel the wind in your hand—
it starts up—

that kind of sad, achy feeling of if you only had a dog.
There is no thing that stops the longing for a dog.

JUMP
to the ceiling!

jump,

Not satellite shoes that
you can wear to **jump,**

Or boots with zippers and all soft fur inside.

Or your very own workbench with real tools,

Not even a grown-up bike
that you can ride everywhere!

No *thing* can stop the longing for a dog because . . .

A thing, no matter how special, is still a *thing*.
A dog is something else.

Once it starts—the longing for a dog—there is no real cure for it.
Not learning to play the trumpet,

Or being vice president of the Tree Climbers Club.

Not going to a monster movie with your best friend
and sharing popcorn, the butter kind,

Not even a whole day
at Howe's Pond can stop
the longing for a dog.

You know, for absolutely sure,
exactly how it would be—
if only you had a dog.

Waking up with a cold, wet nose,
pressing against your face,

Coming home from school to *your* dog
wagging his tail, kissing your nose, and saying
"I LOVE YOU!" in dog language,

Going out in piles of deep, white snow
with *your* dog leaping and bounding

and celebrating all that whiteness!

Going to sleep with *your* dog tucked
right in your bed and dreaming
happy things every night.

But all that knowing is not having,

and nothing can stop
the longing for a dog—

but a DOG!